Zeus and the Skeleton Army

HEROES IN TRAINING

Zeus and the Skeleton Army

By Tracey West

Created by Joan Holub and Suzanne Williams

Aladdin

NEW YORK LONDON TORONTO SYDNEY NEW DELHI

ALADDIN

An imprint of Simon & Schuster Children's Publishing Division
1230 Avenue of the Americas, New York, NY 10020
First Aladdin paperback edition September 2021
Text copyright © 2021 by Joan Holub and Suzanne Williams
Illustrations copyright © 2021 by Craig Phillips
Also available in an Aladdin hardcover edition.
All rights reserved, including the right of reproduction
in whole or in part in any form.
ALADDIN and related logo are registered trademarks of Simon & Schuster, Inc.
For information about special discounts for bulk purchases,
please contact Simon & Schuster Special Sales
at 1-866-506-1949 or business@simonandschuster.com.
The Simon & Schuster Speakers Bureau can bring authors to your live event.
For more information or to book an event
contact the Simon & Schuster Speakers Bureau at 1-866-248-3049
or visit our website at www.simonspeakers.com.
Series designed by Karin Paprocki
Cover designed by Heather Palisi
Interior designed by Mike Rosamilia
The text of this book was set in Adobe Garamond Pro.
Manufactured in the United States of America 0821 OFF
2 4 6 8 10 9 7 5 3 1
Library of Congress Control Number 2021936034
ISBN 9781534432987 (hc)
ISBN 9781534432970 (pbk)
ISBN 9781534432994 (ebook)

⚡ Contents ⚡

Zeus and the Skeleton Army

Greetings,
Mortal Readers,

I t's me, Apollo, the Oracle in Training of Delphi. An oracle is someone who can see the future, and I'm learning to do that. Pythia, the original oracle, is teaching me.

I am not just a fortune-teller in training. I am also an Olympian, the god of music! I play the lyre, and I sing, and I rhyme everything! The other Olympians and I defeated Cronus, and now Zeus sits on Mount Olympus, which is a bonus.

Recently a kid named Hercules and a king named Eurystheus came to Zeus with an argument. Zeus asked me to help solve it. The oracle spoke and said that Hercules had to perform three tasks for the king, and then all would be forgiven.

Zeus decided to help Hercules, and they completed two tasks. Along the way they made some other Olympians angry. Aphrodite, Poseidon, and Hephaestus are upset with Zeus, and now Zeus is upset with Hercules.

Zeus and Hercules are about to embark on their third task. You don't have to be a fortune-teller to know that they're going to make another Olympian angry. Because they're supposed to go to the Underworld and steal from Zeus's brother Hades!

Oh wait—I'm getting a message!

Those who go into the gloom will surely face uncertain doom!

Hmm. Uncertain doom? What does that mean? I guess we will find out soon!

Catch you later, navigator! (Not a bad sign-off, but I'll keep trying.)

CHAPTER ONE

A Ghostly Warning

The soldiers swarmed into the village. Their silver armor gleamed in the sunlight. The screams of the fleeing villagers drowned out their war cries.

Zeus watched from the top of Mount Olympus as the soldiers kept coming . . . and coming . . . and coming . . .

Then the stone underneath Zeus's feet began to shake. The ground cracked and opened wide, and a chariot flew up from the depths of the earth. The rider, a black-haired boy, pointed at Zeus.

"Why have you betrayed me, Brother?"

Zeus bolted upright in bed. Cold sweat covered his arms, and he shivered.

"It was just a dream," he said, but it had felt so real. Too real. And Zeus knew exactly what it meant. He glanced over at the blond-haired boy sleeping on a cot on the other side of the room.

It's all his fault, Zeus thought as he climbed out of bed. *I wouldn't be in this mess if I hadn't agreed to help Hercules.*

Feeling restless, Zeus left the room and began to walk around the temple of the gods. The marble floors felt cool under his bare feet. Suddenly hungry, he made his way to the kitchen, thinking as he walked.

It had all started in his throne room, when Hercules had shown up. Hercules had been followed by his cousin King Eurystheus, who'd been angry at Hercules for throwing stinky monster bird eggs at his palace. Hercules had lied and said that Zeus was his half brother, and so the king had been mad at Zeus, too. Eurystheus had threatened to attack Mount Olympus with his army.

Then Apollo had gotten involved. As the Oracle in Training of Delphi, he had proposed a way to keep the peace. He would consult the oracle, and whatever the forces from beyond suggested, everyone would agree to.

I should have remembered that the forces from beyond don't always make sense, Zeus thought now, scolding himself. He'd reached the temple kitchen, and he shooed a mouse away from a loaf of bread, tore off a chunk, and chewed thoughtfully.

First the oracle had sent Zeus and Hercules to get one of the scales off a sea serpent, then to retrieve a magical belt from the queen of the Amazons. He and Hercules had succeeded, but not without a cost. Zeus's brother Poseidon and some of the other Olympians, Aphrodite and Hephaestus, were pretty angry with him.

"And now Apollo says I need to go to the Underworld and steal Cerberus, who's my brother Hades's favorite pet!" Zeus said out loud, looking at the mouse. "If I steal Cerberus, Hades will be really mad. And if I don't steal Cerberus, King Eurystheus will start a war. I have no idea what to do. Do you?"

The mouse twitched its whiskers in response. Then . . .

Whoosh! An owl swooped past Zeus's face, scooped the mouse up in its claws, and then landed in a corner of the kitchen and gulped the mouse down.

"Hey, Glaukopis, I was talking to him!" Zeus protested.

A brown-haired girl with gray eyes ran in. "Sorry, Zeus," Athena said. "She always gets hungry at night."

Zeus sighed. "It's okay. I'm just trying to figure out what to do about this whole Cerberus thing."

Athena raised an eyebrow. "And you were asking a mouse for advice? When the goddess of cleverness is right here?"

"So, what should I do?" Zeus asked.

Athena yawned. "Let me think about it. My cleverness is not so sharp in the middle of the night."

Zeus nodded. "Okay, thanks. I should get back to bed."

"Come on, Glaukopis!" Athena called, and the owl flew to her outstretched arm.

Zeus walked back to his chamber. When he stepped through the door, he felt a chill. A cold wind swept through the room. He looked to the window, but the curtains hung still.

He frowned. "That's weird."

Suddenly a figure emerged from the shadows in the corner of the room. It looked like a skeleton, but it was also transparent, like a ghost. Its feet floated above the floor, and black mist swirled around its white bones. Zeus tried to scream, but nothing came out. His feet were stuck to the floor.

"Stay away from the Underworld!" the skeleton warned, in a voice that turned Zeus's blood to ice.

A scream finally left his throat. *"Aaaaaaahhhhhhhhhh!"*

CHAPTER TWO

Don't Mess It Up!

The skeletal apparition disappeared. Zeus realized he was shaking.

"Can you quiet down? I'm trying to sleep!" Hercules complained, rolling over on his cot.

"Didn't you see that?" Zeus asked.

"See what? All I see is you standing in the middle of the room when you should be in bed," the boy shot back.

"There was a—a thing," Zeus replied, at a loss for words to describe what he'd seen. "A see-through skeleton wrapped in shadows. Didn't you hear its warning?"

"All I heard was you," Hercules answered. "You must have been dreaming." Then he pulled the blanket over his head.

Zeus looked around the room for any sign of the scary creature but didn't see one. *It might have been a dream,* he thought. *After all, I'd been dreaming about the Underworld just before I woke up. Maybe I've been sleepwalking?*

With that thought comforting him, Zeus got back into bed and fell asleep. He woke a few hours later to sunlight pouring into the room. Across the room Hercules was still asleep, gently snoring.

I can't put off deciding any longer, Zeus thought. *I hope Athena has come up with something!*

He washed up and grabbed some porridge from the kitchen for breakfast—this time with no mice in sight, only the villager who cooked for the Olympians. Then he headed for the throne room.

His sister Hera had been taking his place while he'd been on the road with Hercules. While he'd been away, she had been helping the villagers solve problems about farm animals and property lines and family grudges. She had also decorated the room with peacock feathers on the wall, and a blanket made of peacock feathers on the throne.

"She's sure made herself comfortable," Zeus muttered, sitting down on the throne. It was a great place to think.

Hera strode in, her blond hair coiled on top of her head, and an eyebrow raised at her brother.

"You're still here?" she asked. "I thought you and Muscle Head were supposed to be on the road by now, starting your next quest?"

"I'm not sure if we should go or not," Zeus replied. "If we go, Hades is going to be really angry. If we don't go, there will be a war with King Eurystheus."

Hera put her hands on her hips. "Well, if you're just going to sit here, I guess you've decided not to go."

"That's not true!" Zeus objected, standing. "Athena is going to give me some advice on what to do, and—"

Hera's blue eyes flashed. "Athena? You're asking Athena for advice, while I'm the one who's been here, taking your place, making tough decisions every single day?"

"Well, she is the goddess of cleverness," Zeus shot back.

Hera shook her head. "Fine. Let's see what the brilliant goddess of cleverness has to say."

Just then, Glaukopis flew into the room and landed, perching on top of the throne.

"*Morning-hoo!*" the owl greeted them.

"Good morning, Glaukopis," Zeus said. Hera just scowled at the bird.

Athena strode in. "Zeus, Hera, I've got it!" she cried. "And I didn't even need to use my Thread of Cleverness to help me out."

"Let's hear it," Hera said, her arms folded across her chest.

"Zeus should go to the Underworld," Athena began, "but he shouldn't bring Cerberus back."

"Then why go to the Underworld?" Hera challenged.

"To ask Hades for help," Athena continued. "Zeus, you can ask Hades to return with you and threaten King Eurystheus. The king might want

to take on Mount Olympus, but he probably won't want to mess with the Underworld, too."

Zeus nodded in agreement. "That just might work."

Hercules walked into the room, chomping on an apple, his wavy hair a mess. "Wait, did you just say we should go to the Underworld but *not* bring back the three-headed dog my cousin wants? Can't we just bring Eurystheus the beast?"

"We've been over this," Zeus said. "If we do that, my brother will get really mad. No, I like Athena's plan."

Athena grinned.

"Yay-hoo!" The owl flew off the throne and landed on Athena's arm.

"Well, if Zeus had asked *me* first, I'd have told him the same thing," Hera said. She strolled over to the throne and sat on it.

Glaukopis cocked her head and blinked at Athena. *"Journey-hoo?"*

"Glaukopis thinks we should go with you," Athena said. "I'd like that."

"That would be great!" Zeus said. Athena had always been very helpful to have around when there was trouble.

Hercules flexed his right arm. "And if we get into any danger, I'll protect you."

Athena smiled. "I'm pretty good at taking care of myself. But thanks!"

Hera interrupted them.

"Are you three going to stand here talking all day? I've got villagers who need my *wisdom*." She looked at Athena when she said that last word.

Zeus held up his hands. "Fine. We're leaving."

Hera picked up a staff with a globe on the end that looked like the eye on a peacock feather. She pointed it at them.

"I, Hera, demand that you exit my throne room now!" she ordered in a fancy grown-up voice.

"Seriously?" Zeus asked her.

"No, but that's fun to do," Hera replied in her normal voice. "Just don't mess it up, Thunder-boy. A war on Mount Olympus is the last thing we need."

"Don't worry. We've got this," Zeus replied. "Come on, team!"

Hercules and Athena followed him out of the throne room. Hercules got distracted by look-ing at his reflection in a smooth marble column, and then walked right into the next column.

"Ouch! Who put that there?" he asked angrily, rubbing his head.

Zeus sighed. *I sure* hope *we've got this!*

CHAPTER THREE

The Stinky River

Why do we have to walk everywhere?" Hercules complained as he, Zeus, and Athena made their way up a grassy hillside. "Aren't you, like, the ruler of everything? Shouldn't we be riding in a golden chariot pulled by eagles, or something like that?"

Zeus stopped and turned to face the boy. "Hmm. When would I have time to find a golden chariot? Ever since I became ruler of Mount Olympus, I've been busy solving everyone's problems or babysitting you!"

Hercules flexed his right arm. "Babysitting? I'm no baby! Could a baby do this?"

He walked over to a small tree, wrapped his arms around it, and pulled it out of the ground by the roots.

Zeus shook his head. Hercules had claimed to be half-immortal, but Zeus hadn't believed him at first. However, Zeus had quickly seen that the boy definitely had super strength, so he might have been telling the truth. Hercules's strength was impressive, but he loved showing it off, which was annoying.

Athena raised her eyebrows. "Did you *have* to do that? That was a perfectly nice tree."

"Just making a point," Hercules said, tossing the tree to the side as easily as if it had been an apple. Then he stopped and sniffed the air. "Hey, what's that smell?"

"Stinky-hoo!" Glaukopis agreed.

"It's the River Styx," Athena answered.

"Have you been here before, like I have?" Zeus asked Athena.

She shook her head.

Zeus frowned. "Then how did you know?"

Athena pointed down the hill, to a giant sign that read, RIVER STYX.

They made their way down the hill. Beyond the sign, a brown, sludgy river flowed. Zeus remembered the first time he'd seen it. He'd come with Poseidon and Hades. Zeus hadn't known they were all brothers at the time—and Hades had had no idea that he was the rightful ruler of the Underworld.

Then Zeus remembered something else and stopped.

"Okay, we need to go over a few things. First of all, our magic won't work in the Underworld," he said, patting Bolt, the lightning-bolt-shaped spear tucked into his belt. Each Olympian had at least one magical object, and Bolt was one of Zeus's. At a command, Bolt would grow in size and attack Zeus's enemies—but not once they arrived in the Underworld.

Another of Zeus's magical objects hung around his neck. Chip was an oval stone that helped Zeus by giving him directions. Symbols would appear on Chip, and the stone could even speak in its own special language. But Chip wouldn't work in the Underworld either.

Athena looked down at her cloak. Underneath it she wore the aegis. The shiny metal shield had tassels of pure gold hanging from it.

"I guess we'll have to use our wits, then," she said.

"And our strength!" Hercules added.

"If you *are* half-immortal, then you might not be strong down there," Zeus pointed out.

Hercules flexed again. "This isn't magic. It's muscle."

Athena nodded. "Anything else, Zeus?"

Zeus thought. "Yes," he answered finally. "Once you enter the Underworld, you can't get out. But Hades can overrule that. As long as we don't make *him* angry, he'll allow us to leave. And hopefully, he'll come with us and help us."

Hercules gazed at the river, and at the gray, misty land on the other side. He frowned. "You mean we could be trapped there forever?"

"Not if we stick to the plan," Zeus said. "Now come on, let's get down to the riverbank. Captain Charon is bringing the boat from the other side. Oh, and when he blows the horn, watch out!"

Honk! Charon blew the horn, on cue. *Psst!* A sudden spurt of hot steam sprayed from the ground next to them.

Hercules jumped out of the way. "That's mighty hot! You could have warned us!"

"I just did!" Zeus protested, and he hurried toward the shore before Charon could blow the horn again. Behind him, Zeus heard the owl.

"Flying-hoo!" Glaukopis zoomed past him and landed on a scraggly, leafless tree by the shore.

Honk! Psst! Zeus, Athena, and Hercules hurried to the shore as another puff of steam spurted.

A pale, wrinkled man with long, white hair and wearing a captain's hat called out to them.

"Hallo, young Zeus!" he said. "Have you come to say hello to your old friend Charon?"

The two immortals (and one possibly half-immortal) approached the boat. The smell was worse now that they were close to the water. Glaukopis flew off the tree and landed on Athena's arm.

"Really stinky-hoo!" the owl hooted.

"Hello," Zeus said. "We've actually come to talk to my brother Hades."

Charon nodded. "Aye. But I'll still need to ask for your fare, or that wouldn't be *fair* to everyone else who's dying to get in." He grinned. "Did you hear that? I got two jokes into one sentence."

Zeus had already heard Charon's "dying to get in" joke, but he didn't mention that. Charon was their only way into the Underworld, and Zeus didn't want to insult him. The Olympian reached into his tunic pocket and pulled out three coins.

"I've got the fair fare," he replied, handing the obols to Charon. The boat captain tucked them into a pouch around his waist.

"Fair enough!" Charon said. "And since you're Hades's brother, I won't wait for more passengers. You get the V.I.G. treatment."

"V.I.G.?" Zeus asked.

"Very important gods," Charon replied. Then he narrowed his eyes at Hercules. "Although, I'm not sure if this one is really a god."

"I'm half-immortal!" Hercules boasted.

"Hmpf. Doesn't really matter to me. S'long as you paid." The captain motioned for them to climb onto the boat. "All aboard! One-way trip to eternity!"

"Brace yourselves," Zeus whispered to the others.

"You mean brace ourselves for those weird pink-eyed crocodiles?" Athena asked, motioning toward the creatures surfacing to stare at them from the brown goopy water.

Zeus shook his head. "The crockydeads?

They won't come on board. No, brace yourselves for more of Charon's jokes!"

Charon pushed the flat boat off the shore using the long pole he held. Then he moved the boat slowly through the bubbling, smelly water.

"Zeus, I've got some new jokes," Charon began. "Why is a graveyard so noisy?"

Zeus played along. "I don't know. Why?"

"Because of all the coffins!" Charon replied.

"I don't get it," Hercules said, and Zeus nudged him so he'd be quiet.

"Got anymore?" Zeus asked.

"I've got a million of them!" Charon replied, and Hercules turned to Zeus and made a face. "Why didn't the skeleton eat spicy hummus? Because he didn't have the stomach for it! What kind of key does a ghost use? A spoo-key!"

Charon told joke after joke as they made their way across the river. Only Athena and

Glaukopis seemed to appreciate the captain's sense of humor.

"*Funny-hoo!*" Glaukopis said, and Athena giggled.

"And very clever," she agreed.

Finally they reached the other side of the river. The three travelers climbed off the boat.

"Say hello to your brother for me, Zeus," Charon said. "He hasn't been around to see me in a while."

"Sure," Zeus replied, and then he led the others toward the tall, iron gates leading to the Underworld.

Athena shivered, and Glaukopis ruffled her feathers. "*Creepy-hoo!*"

"Well, I'm not afraid!" Hercules said, but Zeus heard a tremor in his voice. Even so, Hercules boldly strode through the gate first.

Zeus quickly caught up to him. "Let me go

first. Cerberus guards the entrance, and—"

"The three-headed dog?" Hercules asked. He looked around. "I don't see him." Then he pointed. "Is that your brother?"

In the middle of a swamp, just up ahead, sat a magnificent golden throne. A boy wearing a black robe sat on the throne. A golden crown studded with jewels adorned his dark hair.

"Hades!" Zeus cried out, and he ran toward his brother. "It's so good to see you. I'm here to—"

Hades didn't answer. He stared straight ahead, his mouth agape, his eyes blank.

"Yo, Bro!" Zeus said, stepping closer. "It's me, Zeus!"

Hades didn't respond.

"What's the matter with him?" Athena asked after she and Hercules had caught up.

"I'm not sure," Zeus said. Then he remembered his first visit to the Underworld. If you drank the water from a certain river there, you could lose your memory. Was that what had happened to Hades?

"Hades, I can help you," Zeus said. "Just tell me what happened."

Hades still didn't reply. Instead a girl stepped out from behind the throne. She wore a black tunic, and long black hair streamed down her back. Behind her floated see-through skeletons— just like the ones Zeus had seen in his room!

"I am Melinoe," she said. "And you are intruders. Nightmares, capture them!"

CHAPTER FOUR

No Way Out!

A horde of see-through skeletons flew at Zeus, Athena, and Hercules. Zeus's hand reached for Bolt, but it was just a reflex. He knew he couldn't use Bolt.

He tried to grab one of the creature's bony arms. Even though he could see through it, he could touch it. But it felt painfully, icy cold, and Zeus drew back his hand.

Glaukopis flew at one of the Nightmares, and

it plucked the owl out of the air. The owl's body became stiff—as if she were frozen.

"Glaukopis!" Athena shrieked, and she ran toward the owl. Zeus grabbed her arm.

"We can't fight them! We have to run!" he yelled.

Athena paused, glancing at Zeus, but she followed him away from the throne, the Nightmares in pursuit.

Hercules, on the other hand, charged toward the skeletons.

"I'm not afraid of any old bones!" Hercules yelled, throwing wild punches at the creatures. They surrounded him.

Zeus and Athena stopped and looked at each other.

"We can't leave him," Athena said.

Zeus nodded. "I know." And then he ran back toward his brother's throne. Melinoe stood

next to it, calmly watching the scene with glittering black eyes.

"Call off your Nightmares!" Zeus called to her, ducking one of the charging creatures. "And tell me what you've done to my brother!"

Melinoe glared at him. "I don't have to tell you anything."

The ghostly skeletons flew away from Hercules, and the boy stood there, frozen and staring, just like the owl.

"Let's try to grab Hercules," Zeus suggested to Athena. "We can use your cloak to protect us from the Nightmares' touch."

"Clever, Zeus!" Athena responded, and she wrapped Zeus into the cloak with her. Then they ran toward Hercules.

The Nightmares surrounded them, grabbing at Athena's cloak. They pulled it off her. Zeus felt icy hands on his arms. Then everything went black.

He woke up later—how much later, he wasn't sure—in a dreary cave with green slime dripping from the walls. Beetles skittered across the floor, and spiders dangled from the low ceiling. Thick, iron bars blocked the cave entrance.

As his eyes adjusted to the gloom, he saw Athena and Hercules sprawled on the floor next to him. Glaukopis was awake, gently pecking Athena's shoulder. The girl's eyes fluttered open, and she hugged herself, shivering.

"Where are we?" she asked.

"Looks to me like we're in Tartarus," Zeus replied. "It's where Hades locks up the trouble-makers in the Underworld. But I have a feeling Hades isn't in charge anymore."

"Hades looked like he was under a spell," Athena remarked, climbing to her feet. She went over to the bars and pulled on them. "Glaukopis might be able to fit through here. I could send her out to get help."

"I'm not sure where we would send her," Zeus admitted. "She can't leave the Underworld."

Athena bit her lip, thinking. "There's got to be a way out of here."

"No way out!"

"No chance!"

"Trapped forever!"

Zeus recognized those cackling voices coming from outside their prison cell.

"The Furies!" He ran to the bars, hoping to see the three winged women outside. Peering through the bars, he didn't see them.

"Up here!"

The three women were trapped in a cage hanging from the ceiling inside the cell. Each one had black, feathery wings and wild hair. They wore long black dresses and belts made of live snakes. One had a long pointy nose, one wore black pointy boots, and the third one had pointy ears.

"Furies! It's me, Zeus!"

"Hello, brother of Lord Hades," Pointy-Nose replied.

"Hello!" said Pointy-Boots.

"Hello!" echoed Pointy-Ears.

"What are you doing in here?" Zeus asked. "And what happened to Hades? And who is that Melinoe girl?"

"So many questions!" Pointy-Nose said, and cackled.

"Should we tell him?" asked Pointy-Boots.

"He isn't much compared to Lord Hades, but maybe he can help us," said Pointy-Ears.

Pointy-Nose stared at Zeus. "Very well," she said. "Melinoe is the reason why we're here. But she is no girl."

"She is a powerful being," said Pointy-Boots.

"An immortal," added Pointy-Ears.

"Don't interrupt me, Sisters!" Pointy-Nose squawked. "Where was I? Oh yes, Melinoe. She was in a deep sleep for many ages down here, but Hades found her and woke her."

"He thought she was cute," Pointy-Boots chimed in.

"But he didn't realize how dangerous she was," Pointy-Ears finished.

"No, he did not," Pointy-Nose added. "She wants to rule the Underworld. She put one of her Nightmares into Hades's body, and now she controls him."

Zeus remembered Hades's blank face and nodded. "What are those Nightmare things, anyway?"

"Some might call them ghosts," Pointy-Nose answered. "When humans toss off their mortal shell, they come here, to the Underworld. They are shades—pale, shadowy versions of their former selves. But they are not scary."

"No, they're quite boring," Pointy-Boots quipped.

"Annoying," added Pointy-Ears.

"But Melinoe—she believes the dead should join the world of the living—where they do not belong," Pointy-Nose continued. "She releases the shades there and they become Nightmares—ghostly apparitions with dangerous powers."

"We do not agree," said Pointy-Boots.

"We do not approve," added Pointy-Ears.

Zeus remembered the skeleton ghost in the temple, the one who, in his dream prophecy, had warned Zeus not to go to the Underworld. That had to have been one of the Nightmares.

"We tried to defend your brother, and fight Melinoe, but she imprisoned us here," Pointy-Nose explained. "We were on our way to Tartarus to find a ghostberry when her Nightmares defeated us."

Athena piped up. "What's a ghostberry?"

"A white berry that grows in a swamp in Tartarus," Pointy-Nose replied. "They can only be picked by immortals, but if Hades eats one, the berry will cast out the Nightmare inside him."

"And anyone who eats one cannot be harmed by the Nightmares," Pointy-Boots added.

"Then there's hope!" Zeus said. "We just have to get out of here, and—"

"No way out!"

"No chance!"

"Trapped forever!"

"Says who?" Hercules asked. The boy had finally woken up. He strode up to the bars confidently. "Stand back!"

Zeus and Athena exchanged glances, but they obeyed.

It's worth a try, Zeus thought.

Hercules grabbed two of the iron bars and, grunting, slowly pulled them apart. "Told you, it's all muscle!"

He stepped into the gloomy hall outside the cell. Zeus followed, along with Athena, who had Glaukopis on her shoulder.

"Amazing!"

"Impressive!"

"Good work!" the Furies squawked.

Zeus looked up at the swinging cage. "We're going to find the ghostberries. Then we'll save Hades and come back for you."

"Be careful!"

"Be fast!"

"Don't forget us!" Pointy-Ears cried, and Zeus, Athena, and Hercules raced off into the darkness.

CHAPTER FIVE

Into the Gloom

They ran through the dark, slimy corridors of the underground prison.

"It's like a maze!" Hercules complained. "How are we supposed to get out of here?"

Zeus reached for Chip, because the magical talisman would normally tell him which way to go. But he frowned, remembering that his magic didn't work in the Underworld.

Athena pointed to the ground. "We've been

leaving footprints in the damp soil here. As long as we don't see any ahead of us, it means we aren't going around in circles. Let's just keep walking and see where it takes—"

ROOAAAAAAAAAAR!

A loud growl filled the air. Zeus recognized it. "Cerberus?"

He ran toward the sound, and the others followed. Zeus stopped in front of a prison cell containing the enormous three-headed dog with dragon scales covering his body. All three heads growled at Zeus. The creature acted like a sweet little puppy when Hades was around but was naturally hostile to everyone else.

"Cerberus, it's me, Zeus! Hades's brother!" Zeus said. "Did you try to save Hades? Did Melinoe put you in here?"

The heads growled again.

Hercules looked at the beast, wide-eyed.

"This is perfect!" he said. "I can pull open the bars, and then we can take this thing back to my cousin, and Hades will never know."

"NO!" Zeus protested. "That's not the plan. First we need to save my brother from Melinoe, and then we can figure out what to do about King Eurystheus."

Hercules frowned. "If you say so."

Athena ran past them. "Come on, you two. I think I see a way out up ahead."

The boys followed her, and she was right. They emerged from the underground prison cells into a stinky, gloomy landscape. But before they could move forward, giant hands grabbed each one of them from behind!

"*Help-hoo!*" Glaukopis squawked.

Zeus kicked, trying to wriggle out of the giant hand's grasp. Then he found himself staring into two enormous blue eyes that he recognized.

"Briar, it's me, Zeus!" he yelled.

"Just had to make sure," the Titan replied. "It's so gloomy down here that I couldn't see you clearly."

Hercules was punching the giant fist of Kottos, the green-eyed Titan who held him. "Let me go!"

Kottos smiled. "Aren't you cute."

"It's okay!" Zeus called to Hercules and Athena. "They're Titans, but they're my friends. Briar, Kottos, and Gyes are sons of my grandmother Gaia. They live down here so they can guard the other Titans."

The Titans were the very tall immortals who'd once ruled the earth, led by Cronus, Zeus's father. For the most part they were cruel and heartless—and Cronus was the most cruel and heartless of them all.

Zeus and the other Olympians had defeated

them, and now all the bad ones were imprisoned in Tartarus forever. Briar, Kottos, and Gyes were some of the few good ones.

"I'd ask you to put me down, but I think it's easier if we talk face-to-face," Athena told the brown-eyed Gyes, who had her in his grasp. Then she looked down. "Whoa, why do you have so many arms?"

"One hundred, to be exact," Gyes said proudly. "Just like my two brothers."

"Hmph," Hercules said. "Maybe you have one hundred arms, but I have the strength of one hundred arms in just one fist!" He punched Kottos again, and this time the Titan frowned.

"Zeus, who is your little friend here? I don't like him."

"His name is Hercules, and he's why Athena and I are here," Zeus explained. "We came to

talk to Hades, but we found out that he's under the control of Melinoe. Did you know that?"

Briar nodded. "We heard that Hades woke her, but we couldn't do anything to help him. If we leave Tartarus, the other Titans might escape. And that would be bad."

"I understand," Zeus said. "The Furies told us that we could save Hades if we find some ghostberries."

"I know where you can find some," Gyes chimed in. "They grow over by the lava pits. When we put you down, head for the fork in the path. The path on the left will take you to the Elysian Fields, but you need to take the path on the right."

"And don't stray from it!" Kottos warned.

The three Titans gently put Zeus, Athena, and Hercules back on the ground.

"Good. Now I don't have to show you the *real*

power of my mighty fists," Hercules said, and Zeus nudged him.

"Thanks!" Zeus called up to the three hundred-armed giants, and then he, Hercules, Athena, and Glaukopis headed down the path.

The air was chilly and gloomy, and the stinky stench of sulfur grew stronger as they walked. Athena frowned thoughtfully for a while.

"Hercules, it took a lot of strength to bend those bars," she said finally. "Why couldn't you escape from the grasp of that giant?"

Hercules shrugged. "I wasn't really trying."

"I don't believe that," Athena replied. "I think you did try. And I have a theory. Magic for earthly immortals isn't supposed to work down here, right? But you're half-immortal. So maybe your magic works only half the time."

Hercules flexed. "This isn't magic. It's all muscle!"

"Hmm," Zeus said. "You might be right, Athena. I mean, Hercules is strong, but his super strength has always seemed magical to me."

Hercules kicked the damp dirt in front of him. "I could have taken that giant if I'd wanted to," he mumbled.

Zeus suddenly shivered. "Is it getting colder?" he asked. A mist started swirling around them, a mist that suddenly grew thick. Within seconds Zeus couldn't see his hand in front of his face!

"Athena! Hercules!" he called out. But they didn't answer.

Then he heard a voice inside his head.

Come closer, my son!

Zeus gasped. "Cronus!"

CHAPTER SIX

A Blast from the Past

Zeus didn't move. The last time he had seen his father, they had battled for control of Mount Olympus. Zeus had pushed his father into a portal that had sent him to the Underworld to be imprisoned forever. And before that, their relationship hadn't been a great one.

For years Zeus hadn't even known who his father was. Zeus had been raised by a nymph, a goat, and a honeybee. Then he'd learned the truth: Cronus had swallowed (yes, gulped down) Zeus's brothers and sisters because of a prophecy that said one of his children would defeat him. Zeus had escaped the fate of his siblings because his mom, Rhea, had fed Cronus a stone instead of baby Zeus, and had given Zeus to the nymph and animals, to be raised by them.

But Zeus had discovered his destiny, and his magical weapons, and had released his brothers and sisters from Cronus's big belly. Then the war for Mount Olympus had begun. And now . . .

The fog cleared, and Zeus found himself in front of an enormous stone cube. It was as tall as a Titan and just as wide.

"Cronus?" Zeus asked.

My son! Cronus said. *Have you come to free me?*

Zeus heard the voice in his head again. He

figured that somehow Cronus was trapped inside the huge block of stone.

"Why would I do that?" he asked.

You have proven yourself to be a worthy warrior, Cronus replied. *I would expect nothing less from a son of mine. But how are you using your power? You roam the land like a vagabond while your sister sits on your throne!*

"I'm roaming the land to avoid a war!" Zeus shot back.

There is no honor in running from war! Cronus replied. *Free me, my son, and we will smite your enemies together. We will reclaim your throne . . .*

Zeus squeezed his eyes shut, willing the voice in his head to go away. Cronus had always wanted Zeus to join him, and Zeus had never given in. But Cronus was great at filling Zeus's head with doubts. This errand with Hercules had been nothing but trouble. And Hera was getting very comfortable on his throne. . . .

"GET OUT OF MY HEAD!" Zeus yelled, and his voice boomed like thunder. A tiny crack appeared in the stone block.

That's it, my son. Release your anger.

"I said, GET OUT OF MY HEAD!" His voice boomed again, and another crack appeared.

Zeus felt a hand on his shoulder—a regular-size hand, not a giant one. Athena pulled him away from the stone.

"We've got to get back onto the path, Zeus!" she said.

"Path-hoo!"

They broke into a run and arrived back at the path, panting. Zeus paused, listening. But his father's voice was gone.

"Thanks," he said. "How did you find me?"

"Glaukopis has amazing senses," Athena

replied. "She found you through the mist. What was that all about?"

"Cronus," Zeus replied. "But that's behind us now. Let's go find those ghostberries!"

He started to charge ahead, but then stopped. "Wait, where's Hercules?"

Athena shrugged. "I lost him in the mist too, but Glaukopis says she can't see or hear him. Maybe he went on ahead to find the berries?"

"Maybe," Zeus agreed. "Let's find him before he discovers a way to mess everything up."

They ran down the path until they came to a big, bubbling pool of lava.

"Gyes said something about lava," Zeus said. He looked around. "No sign of Hercules. And where are the berries?"

Athena squinted across the lava pool. "Looks like there's an island in there. See the bush growing from it?"

Zeus peered across the lava and spotted it. "Oh, great!" he said. "It's too bad we can't send Glaukopis to get the ghostberries for us. But they have to be retrieved by an immortal."

Then Zeus noticed stones jutting out of the lava—a lot of them. All he and Athena would have to do was jump from stone to stone, and they'd reach the island. He started to leap to the first stone, but Athena grabbed him and pulled him back.

"Don't do it!" she warned.

CHAPTER SEVEN

Ghostberries

Why did you pull me back? We need to get to the berries," Zeus said.

"I think there's a pattern," Athena said. "Look, some of the stepping stones are round. And some of them are square. I think you need to step on certain stones to get across."

Zeus frowned. "How do we know which ones to step on?"

Athena picked up a small rock from the

ground. She tossed it onto the first stone, a round one. The stone sank into the lava, and the hot, orange liquid bubbled loudly.

Zeus's eyes got wide. "Okay, so not that one."

"Let's try a square one," Athena suggested, and this time Zeus threw the rock onto a square stone. The rock landed on the stepping stone, which did not move.

"So we jump on only the square stones?" Zeus asked.

"I think so," Athena replied. "But let's bring some rocks with us to make sure."

"Meet you—hoo!" Glaukopis said, and she flew across the lava and landed on the bush.

Zeus and Athena made their way across the stepping stones as the lava hissed and bubbled all around them. They tested each square stone with a rock first, and none of the square stones sank. They had figured out the trick to get across.

Finally they landed on the island. A single, large bush grew in the middle of the rocky island. The prickly leaves were such a dark green, they looked black. A single cluster of eight berries grew from one of the branches. Zeus reached to pick them, and then stopped.

"Do you think it's safe?" he asked Athena.

"I don't see anything that looks like a trap," she replied, and Zeus plucked the berries. He kept four and gave the rest to Athena.

"Thanks," she said. "We have to make sure to save one for Hades."

Zeus looked at the white berries in his hand. "Should we eat one now?"

Athena gazed around. "Maybe we should wait until we encounter the Nightmares again. We don't know how long the powers of the berries are supposed to last."

They jumped back across the steaming lava

pit, one stone at a time. Then they retraced the route they'd taken to get there.

"Do you know how to get back to Hades's throne?" Athena asked.

"Let's go back to the fork," Zeus suggested. "Gyes said the other path would take us to the Elysian Fields, and from there we can get to Hades's throne. I remember from the first time I came here."

Athena nodded. "Okay. But let's stick together, in case another mist comes up."

She held out her hand, and Zeus took it. They made their way down the gloomy trail once more.

"I wonder what happened to Hercules," Athena mused.

"*Lost-hoo!*" Glaukopis guessed.

"Well, I hope he's okay," Zeus said. "And once we get Hades back, he'll be able to help us find

Hercules. Hades knows everything that happens here in the Underworld."

No thick fog stopped them from reaching the fork in the path, and they took it toward the Elysian Fields. With each step they took, the darkness and gloom lifted a little bit. And the stinky stench became much less stinky.

Soon they reached a meadow dotted with millions of white flowers.

Athena stopped. "This is beautiful!"

"Pretty-hoo!" Glaukopis agreed.

"It's Asphodel Meadow," Zeus explained. "It's one of the nicer places in the Underworld. Most people are sent here or to the Elysian Fields when they die."

"So the good ones go here, and the bad ones go to Tartarus," Athena said, and Zeus nodded. Athena looked up. "It's sunny here, but I don't see any sun."

"Underworld magic," Zeus replied. He sniffed the air. "But the nice smell of the flowers, that's real."

"Much better than the stinky stench we left behind us," Athena agreed.

They let go of each other's hands and walked across the meadow until they saw a thick, green hedge that stretched as far as they could see.

"That's the entrance to the Elysian Fields!" Zeus announced.

They reached the door five minutes later. A sign on it read:

REAR ENTRANCE OF THE ELYSIAN FIELDS WHERE EVERYONE IS GOOD, AND DEAD

"Clever," Athena said.

"Funny-hoo!" agreed Glaukopis.

Zeus pushed open the door and they went inside. In front of them stretched enormous fields filled with the most beautiful things:

grapevines, fruit trees, flowers, and bubbling fountains. Pale people walked among the plants, talking and laughing.

Athena's eyes got wide. "They look—alive."

Zeus nodded. "They're shades of their former selves," he said, remembering the Furies' explanation.

Suddenly the light dimmed in the Elysian Fields. A cold wind whipped up, and Athena's cloak billowed and flapped.

"Zeus, I think it's time for the berries!" she cried.

Athena and Zeus reached for the berries in their pockets and swallowed one each. Then Athena fed one to Glaukopis.

"Are we supposed to feel different?" Zeus wondered. "I don't feel anything."

A loud screech filled the fields, and a small army of Nightmares sped toward them, flying in the air. Zeus and Athena faced them.

The Furies said that the Nightmares couldn't hurt us if we ate the berries, Zeus remembered. *I hope they're right!*

Then he looked over at Athena—and gasped! The girl and the owl on her shoulder were both see-through. He looked down at his body. He was see-through too!

"The ghostberries have turned us into ghosts!" he yelled.

CHAPTER EIGHT

Nightmare Attack!

I guess that's why they're called ghostberries!" Athena quipped. "I think this means we're on the same level as the ghosts now."

To test her theory she kicked her legs, and her body floated upward. She grinned. "Cool!"

Zeus did the same. It felt weird, to be floating in the air! But he had other things to worry about. The Nightmares had almost reached them.

"How do we fight them?" he wondered.

Athena took off her aegis and tapped the gold shield. It made a metallic sound.

"My plan is to whack them over the head with this," she said. "And also—Glaukopis, peck them!"

The owl screeched and flew toward the attacking Nightmares. Zeus balled his hands into fists.

"I don't think we can fight them all," he called to Athena. "Let's just try to get through them to the front gate of the Elysian Fields, so we can get to Hades."

Athena nodded. "Good strategy!" Then she held the shield in front of her face and launched herself forward through the air. There was a *clank* of metal against bone as her shield hit an oncoming Nightmare, and the skeleton dropped to the ground.

Now that we're ghosts, the Nightmares feel solid,

Zeus realized. He flew forward, trying to zig-zag between the attackers, since he didn't have a weapon.

He felt a bony hand grab his ankle, jerking him back down to the ground.

At least I'm not frozen this time! Zeus thought, and he kicked as hard as he could. The Night-mare lost its grip, and then flew in front of Zeus to face him. The Nightmare's hideous, toothy grin sent a ripple of fear through Zeus. He pushed the fear aside.

"Aaaaaahhhhhh!" With a cry, Zeus attempted to charge past the Nightmare. The creature grabbed him by the arm and flipped him over. Zeus gave a mighty push, and the Nightmare tumbled off him. Zeus launched himself into the air again.

Up ahead he saw Glaukopis pecking at the attackers, keeping them busy as Athena forged

ahead with her shield. Zeus moved to catch up to her, but two Nightmares came at him from the right and the left. He quickly ducked, and the two creatures crashed into each other.

Zeus zipped forward. Another Nightmare charged toward him, and Zeus grabbed its bony arm and tossed the creature aside.

He caught up to Athena just as the door in the green hedge came into view. It was open—and more Nightmares were streaming through it.

Athena glanced at Zeus, worried. "There are too many of them!" she said, slamming her shield into another Nightmare.

"I'll try to distract them," Zeus told her. "Get to the throne and feed Hades one of those berries."

Athena nodded. "I'll try."

Clank! Clank! Clank! She forged ahead, and the Nightmares swarmed her.

"Hey, boneheads!" Zeus yelled. "Betcha can't catch me!"

Thirteen empty skulls turned toward Zeus. Their eye sockets locked on him. Zeus flew over to an apple tree and perched in the branches there.

"Come and get me, numbskulls!" he taunted.

The Nightmares zoomed toward him, and Zeus realized he didn't have a plan. He grabbed a nearby apple and chucked it at the Nightmares.

Thonk! It hit one right in the skull, sending the Nightmare spiraling across the field.

"Nice!" Zeus cheered. He picked two more apples.

Thonk! Thonk!

He knocked down two more Nightmares. But more kept coming. Their bony fingers gripped his arms and legs. They pulled him out of the tree.

"Hey, watch it!" Zeus cried.

The Nightmares flew toward the exit, carry-ing Zeus. He watched as the white ghostberries fell out of his pocket onto the green field below.

I hope Athena has made it, he thought.

The Nightmares carried him out of the Ely-sian Fields and back to Hades's golden throne. Hades still sat there, blank-eyed. Melinoe stood next to him with Athena, whose body looked solid again. *The berry's powers must have worn off!* Zeus guessed. He looked down at his own body and saw that he was solid too.

But that wasn't all that was different about Athena. She floated next to Melinoe, wrapped in a shroud of black mist.

"Sorry, Zeus," Athena said as the Nightmares placed him in front of Melinoe. "She used some kind of weird magic on me."

"That's okay," Zeus said, but it was definitely *not* okay. He tried to think. He couldn't help

Hades, because he didn't have any more berries. He'd have to free Athena. And that meant fighting Melinoe.

"Let's battle, me and you," he said to Melinoe. "If I win, you let Athena go."

Melinoe grinned. "Why do boys always want to fight?" She pointed both hands at Zeus, and black mist streamed from her fingers. He breathed it in, and a feeling of despair came over him.

My father was right! he thought. *I'm supposed to be a powerful ruler, but I'm not. I'm a failure. I'll never be able to rule Mount Olympus.*

That's not true. A teeny voice inside him fought back, but the feeling of misery was much stronger. Zeus lost his will to stand up to Melinoe.

What's the point?

The mist wrapped around Zeus, lifting him off the ground. Melinoe snapped her fingers, and two Nightmares floated over. One hovered in front of Athena's face, and the other in front of Zeus's face.

"Now open wide," Melinoe said, and Zeus felt his mouth open involuntarily.

The teeny voice inside him spoke up again. *Don't let her do it! You'll be like Hades! Under her control forever!*

But it was no use. Zeus couldn't close his mouth. The Nightmare flew toward him . . .

"Hades-hoo!"

Glaukopis appeared, and landed on Hades's shoulder. She coughed, and a white berry appeared in her beak.

She dropped it into Hades's mouth.

CHAPTER NINE

Large and In Charge

Hades swallowed the berry. A second later his mouth opened wide and a Nightmare flew out, shrieking.

Hades's brown eyes began to shimmer. He stood up, and his body grew to three times its normal size. His voice exploded from his mouth.

"NIGHTMARES, BEGONE!"

Compelled by the ruler of the Underworld, the Nightmares instantly disappeared. But

Athena and Zeus remained trapped in Melinoe's mist. The girl faced Hades, and the smile had faded from her face.

"Hades, I can explain—"

"RELEASE THEM!" Hades boomed, and Zeus was impressed. His brother's angry voice rivaled Zeus's thunder voice.

Melinoe's eyes narrowed. "I have something you want. Let's make a deal, then."

"NO DEAL!" Hades yelled. "MY FURIES, GRAB HER!"

Melinoe smiled thinly. "You've been under my powers for too long, Hades. I have locked up anyone who is loyal to you. Now step away from the throne, and I will spare your friends."

As she spoke, the earth underneath them all began to rumble. Pointy-Nose, Pointy-Boots, and Pointy-Ears shot up through a hole in the ground, cackling.

Melinoe stared at them, wide-eyed. "How did you get out?"

"Muscle Boy set us free," answered Pointy-Nose.

"And now here we are," continued Pointy-Boots.

"For revenge!" added Pointy-Ears with a cackle.

The three Furies swooped down onto Melinoe and plucked her up with their claws. Then they carried her back down through the hole.

Zeus and Athena thudded to the ground, freed from the black mist. Zeus jumped to his feet and ran to Hades. The boy shrank back down to the size of a human, and the glow faded from his eyes.

"Zeus!" he cried, and the brothers hugged.

Glaukopis landed on Athena's shoulder, and they joined the boys. Hades patted the fluffy head of the owl.

"I owe your little friend here some thanks," Hades said. "It's no fun having a weird ghost creature living inside you."

Zeus turned to Athena. "Where did Glaukopis get that berry from, anyway?"

"Owls can't chew their food," Athena answered. "She must have coughed it up from her gizzard."

"Gizzard-hoo!" Glaukopis confirmed.

Hades made a face. "So that was an owl-puke berry?"

Zeus slapped him on the back. "Well, it saved you from Melinoe!" he said. "Do you want to tell us how she ended up taking over things? The Furies told us that she was asleep and you woke her up."

Hades shrugged. "Everyone said she was dangerous, but I've been pretty lonely down here," he said. "Anyone who serves me is, like, thousands of years old, and I miss being around kids my own age. You and Athena and everyone else. I thought maybe Melinoe could be my friend."

"But she was as dangerous as they said," Athena pointed out.

Hades sighed. "Yeah, I know. Guess it's back to being lonely on my throne." Then he brightened. "Wait, I've got you two! Did you just come down here to visit? Or are you going to stay awhile?"

Zeus explained their mission to Hades. He started his story with the day when Hercules had first shown up in the temple throne room, and he ended with Hercules disappearing into the mist.

"He probably just got lost," Zeus finished. "But I figured, with your all-knowing Underworld powers, you could find him, and then you could come back with us so we can scare King Eurystheus and end this whole thing."

"Sure. Let's go rescue Cerberus first, though," Hades said. "My poor puppy must be so scared and lonely. He probably doesn't even have any treats down there."

He nodded over to a pile of giant bones, which Zeus guessed must have been treats for the giant three-headed dog.

Zeus nodded. "He's locked up in Tartarus. We can—"

"Easy, boy, easy!"

Suddenly Hercules appeared, riding Cerberus! The boy had fashioned reins out of chains—chains that looked like they'd come from the cage holding the Furies.

"Hey, let go of my dog!" Hades yelled.

All three heads snapped toward their master, whining. But Hercules was controlling them with his brute strength. Frightened and confused, the dog bounded forward, toward the River Styx.

"Chariot!" Hades cried, clapping his hands,

and instantly a chariot drawn by four black horses appeared. Hades, Zeus, and Athena jumped on.

"Away! Catch up to Cerberus!" Hades cried, and the horses took off after Hercules and the three-headed dog.

CHAPTER TEN

Hera's Proclamation

The four black horses pulling the chariot quickly caught up to Hercules and Cerberus. The dog's three heads turned to Hades again, whimpering. Hercules pulled on the chains, trying to steer them away.

But Cerberus pulled with all his might, breaking the chains! The dog jumped onto the back of the chariot, causing the nose of the cart to tip toward the gloomy sky. The chariot shot up, and Zeus and Athena grabbed on to the seat to keep from falling off. Down below rolled the muddy brown waters of the River Styx.

"Hades, what's happening?" Zeus yelled.

"I'm trying to shake off Hercules!" his brother responded.

Hercules had slipped off Cerberus, but now he clung to one of the chariot wheels. His body and legs dangled in the air.

"Turn back!" Zeus yelled.

"Too late now!" Hades yelled.

The chariot flew up into the thick, gray clouds above the river. Zeus shivered. Then . . .

Bam! They crash-landed onto a patch of green grass. Overhead the sun shone in a bright blue sky. They were back in the world. But where were they?

Zeus turned to see the white, gleaming marble temple of the oracle. The sound of Apollo's lyre and voice streamed out from inside.

"Listen, oh king, what do you hear?
The dog that you desire is near!"

King Eurystheus, a burly man in a red robe, with bushy black hair and a bushy black beard, ran out of the temple. His eyes lit up. Behind him came Apollo, a golden-haired boy wearing a white tunic.

"Cerberus, the three-headed guardian of the Underworld!" King Eurystheus cried. "He is mine!"

Hades climbed down from the chariot. "Don't even think about it!" he said. "I came to tell you that there is no way you're going to get my dog. He's mine!"

Hercules detached himself from the wheel. "I brought him to you, Cousin. What happens now is up to you! A deal's a deal, and I'm off the hook."

King Eurystheus frowned. "I don't think it counts. You were just supposed to bring me the dog, not Hades, too."

"Well, the oracle didn't say I *shouldn't* bring Hades," Hercules pointed out, looking at Apollo.

The king stepped toward Cerberus. "Here, boy. Do you want to come home with your new daddy?"

All three heads of the dragon dog growled, and King Eurystheus frowned. He turned to Apollo. "This doesn't seem right at all."

"The rules are clear; the dog is here," Apollo said with a shrug.

The king stomped his foot. "This isn't fair!"

Zeus stomped up to Hercules. "This is all your fault! We had a plan! Why won't you ever *listen?*"

"I just wanted to get my cousin off my back," Hercules said. "Besides, *my* plan worked.

Cerberus is here, and Hades isn't angry with you, and now all the tasks are over."

"Hardly!" King Eurystheus cried, his face turning as red as his robes. "Oracle, I demand another quest, or I shall go to war!"

"Oh yeah? Well, do you really want to go to war with Mount Olympus *and* the Underworld?" Zeus shot back, putting his original plan into motion.

Hades held up both hands. "Wait a second. I don't want to go to war."

"But we saved you from Melinoe!" Zeus cried. "Can't you please help us out with this?"

"You also brought this dog stealer into my land," Hades said, nodding toward Hercules.

Zeus faced Hercules. "See? You ruin *everything*!"

A hurt look crossed the boy's face, and Zeus felt bad—for a split second. Because then a boy wearing winged sandals flew down from the

sky. It was Hermes, an Olympian and the offi-
cial messenger of the gods.

"I have a proclamation from Hera of Mount
Olympus," Hermes said, unrolling a scroll of paper.
Then he cleared his throat and read in a loud voice.

> "*I, Hera of Mount Olympus, do
> formally claim the throne of Mount
> Olympus.*
>
> *My brother Zeus is no longer
> welcome here.*
>
> *Why? I looked into the eye of my
> magical peacock feather, and it showed
> me what is to come. Zeus will only
> bring war and disaster to the land. So
> if you see him, tell him to scram!*"

Hermes rolled up the scroll. Everyone stared
at Zeus.

"But she—she can't do that!" Zeus protested. "I'm the ruler of the gods! None of this is my fault! And anyway, we need to stick together, right?"

"Excellent! My enemy has been weakened!" King Eurystheus said. He nodded to Hades. "Keep your dog. I'm going to assemble my troops!"

He marched off.

Zeus looked at Athena. "Can you talk some sense into our sister?"

Athena frowned. "I'll try. I may be clever, but she is very smart. Which I think beats clever."

Athena headed off, and Zeus addressed Apollo. "What's going to happen? What should I do? I'm so confused!"

"Follow me, and I'll consult the mists," Apollo said.

Hermes lifted up. "Later, Zeus! I'll tell Hera you got the message," he said cheerfully.

"And I'm going to get back to the Underworld and feed Cerberus," Hades said, scratching the three heads. "My widdle buddy needs his din-din."

He climbed back onto the chariot, and Cerberus jumped on behind him.

"I *am* grateful that you and Athena saved me, Zeus," Hades said. "It wasn't easy being under Melinoe's control. I was even starting to miss Charon's jokes. What is a king's favorite weather?"

"I don't know," Zeus replied.

"Hail!" Hades cried. "Away, chariot!"

The chariot disappeared back into the Underworld, and Zeus smiled. Even though everything was a big mess, it was good to see his brother back to normal.

Zeus climbed up the steps into the temple, and Hercules followed him.

"Don't you have somewhere else to be?" Zeus asked.

"Not really," Hercules replied, and he sounded so sad that Zeus didn't have the heart to send him away. They found Apollo in front of a pool of water with a light mist floating on top. Apollo stared into the mist.

"What do you see?" Zeus asked eagerly.

Apollo strummed his lyre. Then he sang:

> *"There will be loss, and there will be gain.*
>> *But one thing is sure. Chaos will reign!"*

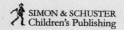

READ & LEARN

with

simon kids

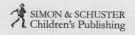

Goddess Girls

READ ABOUT ALL YOUR FAVORITE GODDESSES!

**#16 MEDUSA
THE RICH**

**#17 AMPHITRITE
THE BUBBLY**

**#18 HESTIA
THE INVISIBLE**

**#19 ECHO
THE COPYCAT**

**#20 CALLIOPE
THE MUSE**

**#21 PALLAS
THE PAL**

**#22 NYX
THE MYSTERIOUS**

**#23 MEDEA
THE ENCHANTRESS**

EBOOK EDITIONS ALSO AVAILABLE

From Aladdin
simonandschuster.com/kids

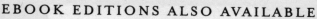